Put Beginning Readers on the Right Track with
ALL ABOARD READING™

The All Aboard Reading series is especially for beginning readers. Written by noted authors and illustrated in full color, these are books that children really and truly *want* to read—books to excite their imagination, tickle their funny bone, expand their interests, and support their feelings. With four different reading levels, All Aboard Reading lets you choose which books are most appropriate for your children and their growing abilities.

Picture Readers—for Ages 3 to 5
Picture Readers have super-simple texts with many nouns appearing as rebus pictures. At the end of each book are 24 flash cards—on one side is the rebus picture; on the other side is the written-out word.

Level 1—for Preschool through First Grade Children
Level 1 books have very few lines per page, very large type, easy words, lots of repetition, and pictures with visual "cues" to help children figure out the words on the page.

Level 2—for First Grade to Third Grade Children
Level 2 books are printed in slightly smaller type than Level 1 books. The stories are more complex, but there is still lots of repetition in the text and many pictures. The sentences are quite simple and are broken up into short lines to make reading easier.

Level 3—for Second Grade through Third Grade Children
Level 3 books have considerably longer texts, use harder words and more complicated sentences.

All Aboard for happy reading!

To my wife, Georgia, for her support—N.N.

To my mother who, in life, gave nothing but love, understanding, and encouragement—M.D.R.

Special thanks to Dr. Edmond A. Mathez, Associate Curator, Department of Earth and Planetary Sciences, American Museum of Natural History, New York.

Library of Congress Cataloging-in-Publication Data

Nirgiotis, Nicholas.
   Volcanoes : mountains that blow their tops / by Nicholas Nirgiotis ; illustrated by Michael Radencich.
     p.   cm. — (All aboard reading)
   "Level 2, grades 1-3."
   Summary: Describes the formation and activities of volcanoes and identifies some notable eruptions.
   1. Volcanoes—Juvenile literature. [1. Volcanoes.] I. Radencich, Michael, ill. II. Title. III. Series.
QE521.3.N557   1996
551.2'1—dc20
                                               95-22045
                                              CIP
ISBN 0-448-41144-X (GB) A B C D E F G H I J   AC

ISBN 0-448-41143-1 (pbk) A B C D E F G H I J

ALL
ABOARD
READING™
Level 2
Grades 1-3

Volcanoes
Mountains That Blow Their Tops

By Nicholas Nirgiotis
Illustrated by Michael Radencich

Grosset & Dunlap • New York

It is a quiet day on an island.

Or so it seems.

Suddenly a mountain starts to shake.

Clouds of smoke shoot from the top.

The mountain smokes for days and days.

Then it happens!

KABOOM!

The mountain blows its top!

A red-hot cloud of ash bursts out.

It burns the town in minutes.

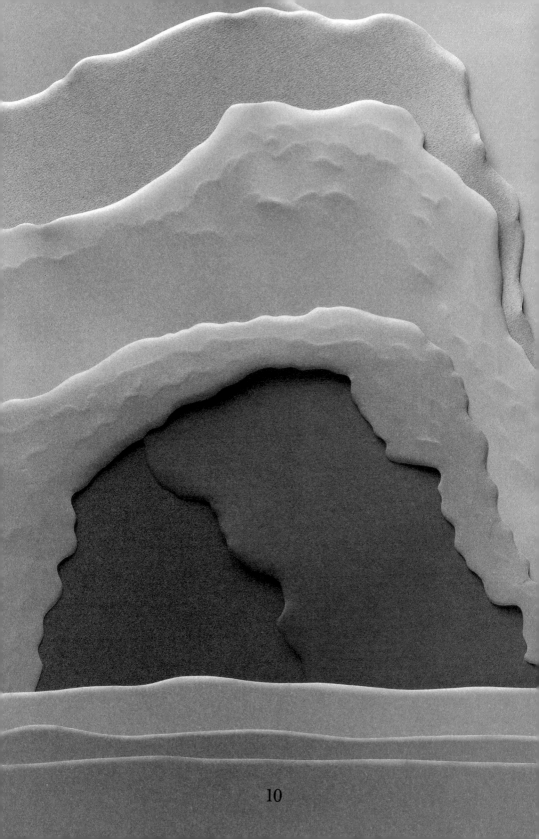

Just two people get away.

One is a girl.

She knows a cave.

She used to play there.

She takes a boat to the cave.

She is safe.

The other is a man.

He is safe in a jail

underground.

This is a true story.

It happened in 1902.

Mont Pelée is the name

of the mountain.

(You say it like this:

mont pe-LAY.)

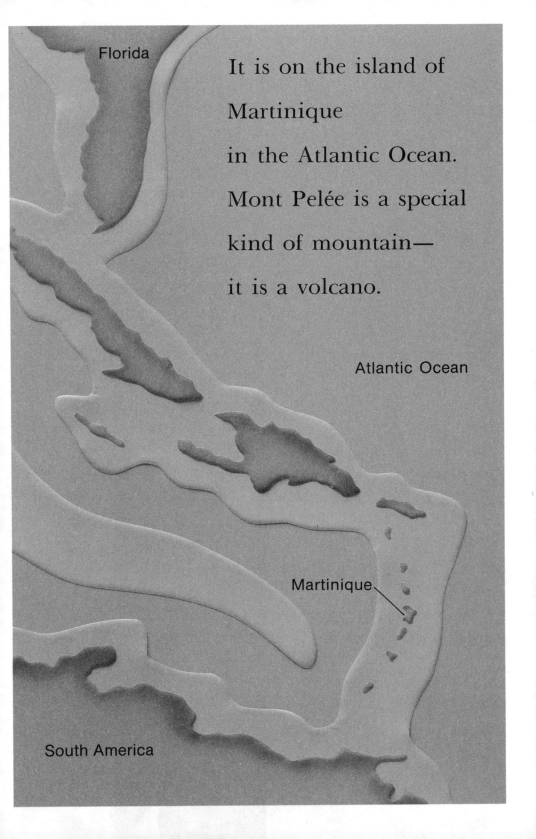

Florida

It is on the island of
Martinique
in the Atlantic Ocean.
Mont Pelée is a special
kind of mountain—
it is a volcano.

Atlantic Ocean

Martinique

South America

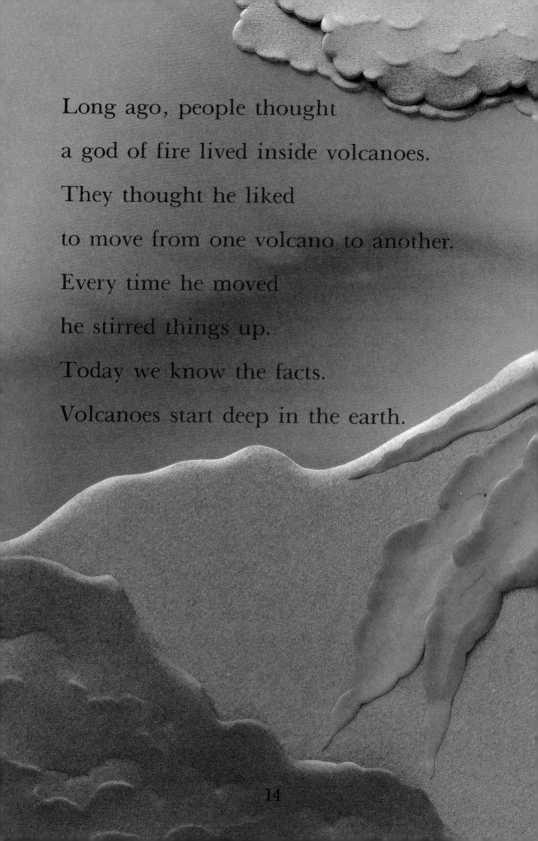

Long ago, people thought
a god of fire lived inside volcanoes.
They thought he liked
to move from one volcano to another.
Every time he moved
he stirred things up.
Today we know the facts.
Volcanoes start deep in the earth.

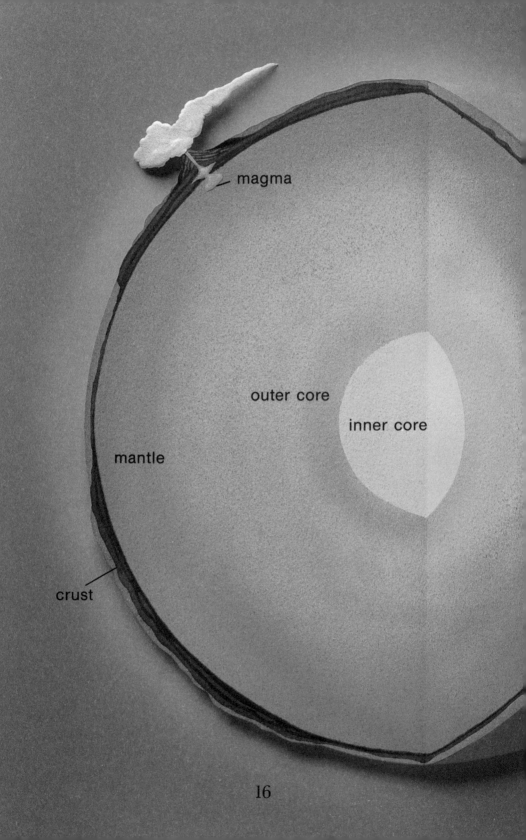

magma

outer core

inner core

mantle

crust

The earth is round—
like an orange.
It is made of layers
of rock.
The top layer is called
the crust.
It is like the skin
of the orange.
The layer below
is called the mantle.
The mantle is very hot.
So some of the rock melts.
The melted rock is
called magma.

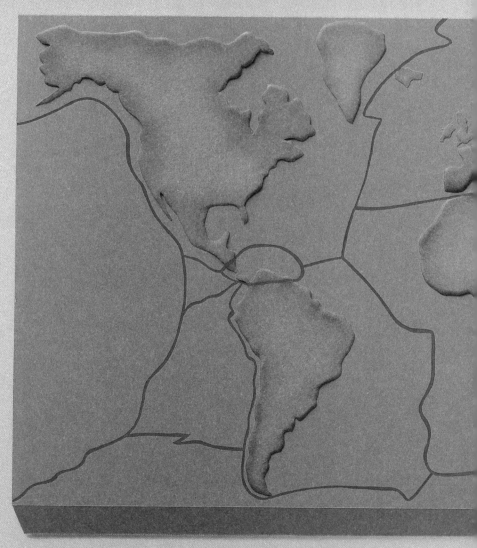

The top layers of earth are made up

of many pieces.

These pieces are called plates.

The red lines show where the plates meet.

This is where most volcanoes happen.

The plates are always moving—

very, very slowly!

Some plates push against each other.

Some plates pull away

from each other.

The magma is moving too.

It pushes up on the plates.

Sometimes the magma

finds a crack

between the plates.

Then—SPURT!

Out it comes.

This is the start

of a volcano.

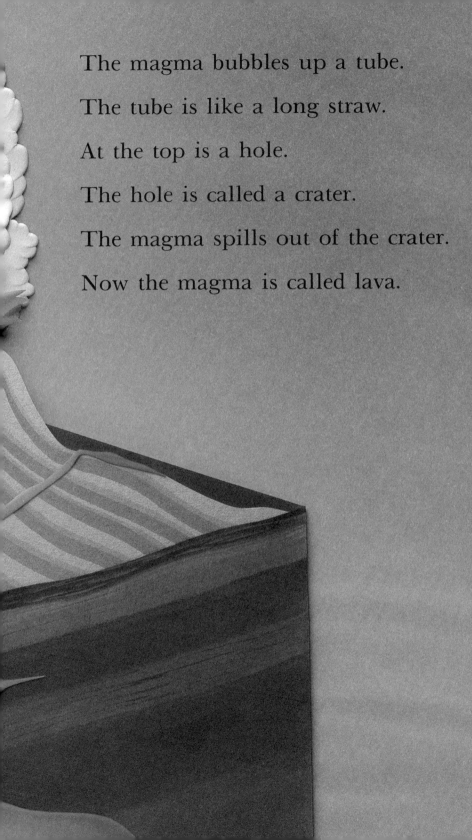

The magma bubbles up a tube.

The tube is like a long straw.

At the top is a hole.

The hole is called a crater.

The magma spills out of the crater.

Now the magma is called lava.

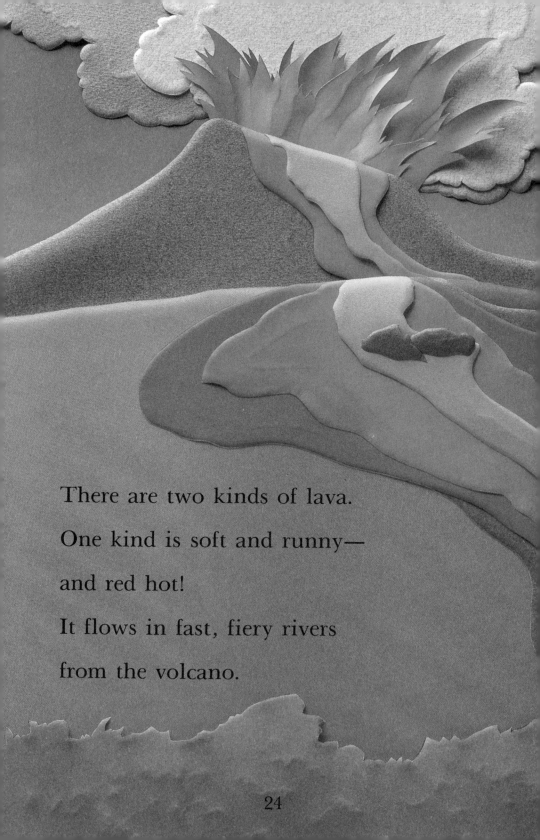

There are two kinds of lava.

One kind is soft and runny—

and red hot!

It flows in fast, fiery rivers

from the volcano.

As the lava cools,

it turns back into smooth rock.

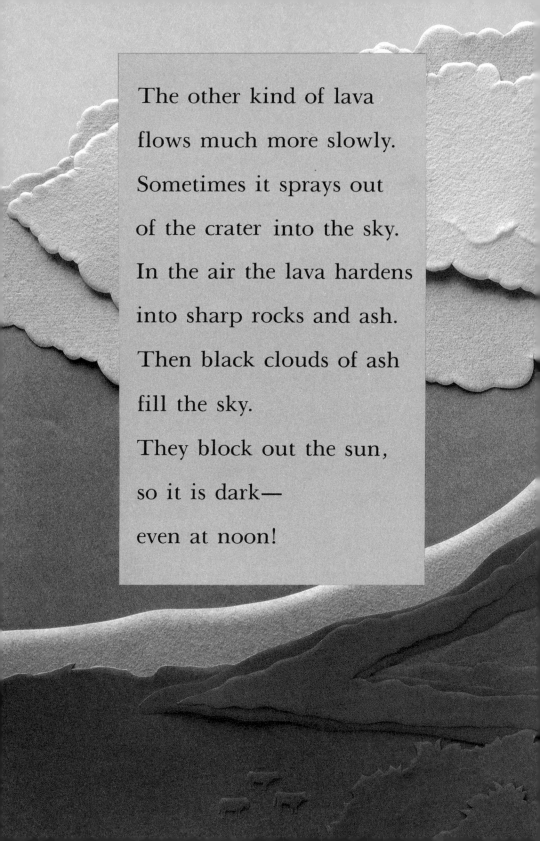

The other kind of lava
flows much more slowly.
Sometimes it sprays out
of the crater into the sky.
In the air the lava hardens
into sharp rocks and ash.
Then black clouds of ash
fill the sky.
They block out the sun,
so it is dark—
even at noon!

Not many people get to see

a volcano being born.

But fifty years ago,

one boy did.

He lived in Mexico.

One day he was helping

his father on their farm.

Suddenly the earth split open.

Smoke and ash shot into the air.

The boy and his father ran

to warn the people in town.

Ash and rock kept shooting up.

A hill started to grow.

By the next day,
the hill was as tall
as ten houses.

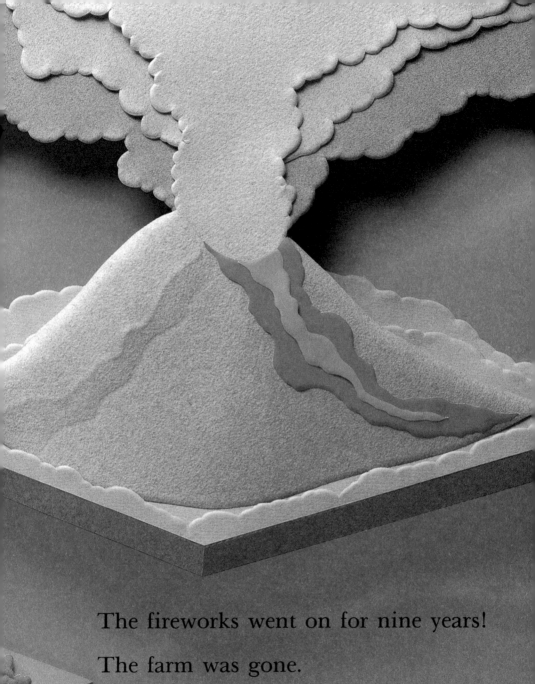

The fireworks went on for nine years!

The farm was gone.

The town was gone.

In their place was a new volcano.

Some volcanoes start
at the bottom of the sea,
where no one can see them.
The ocean floor splits open.
Hot lava pours out.

The lava cools and hardens.

The volcano grows.

Slowly it rises above the water.

This is how some islands are made.

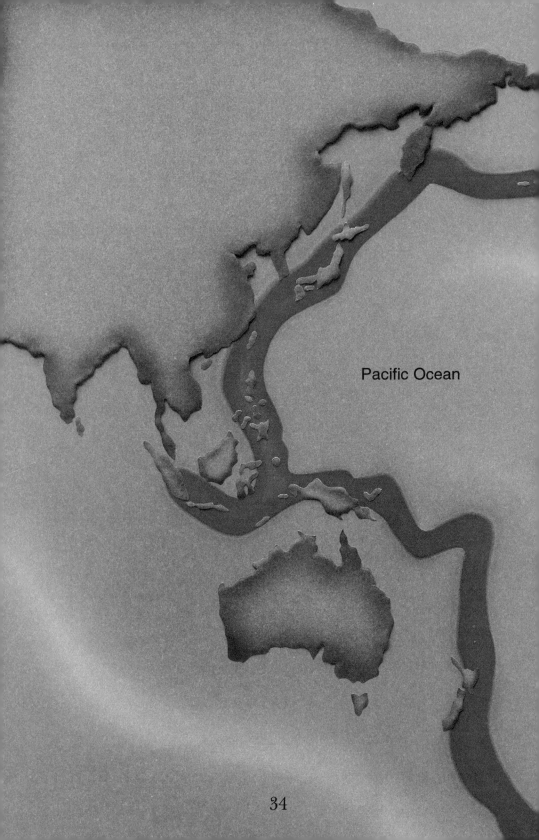

Pacific Ocean

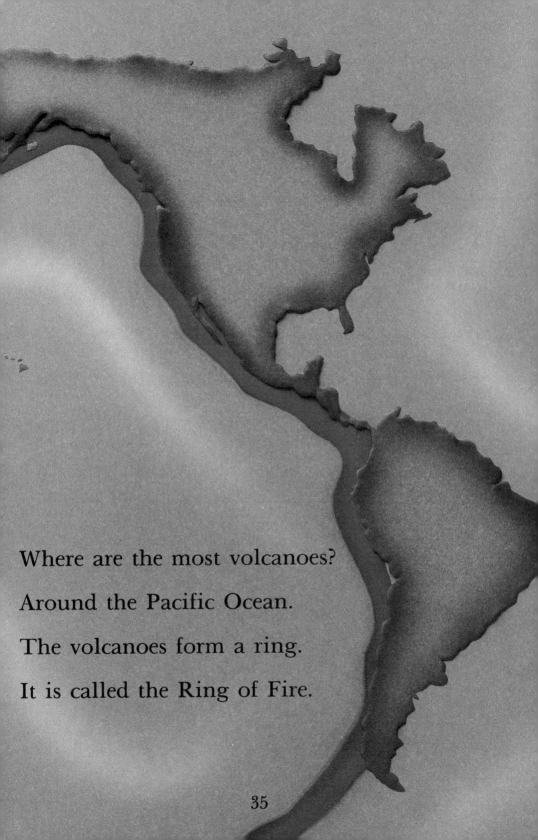

Where are the most volcanoes?

Around the Pacific Ocean.

The volcanoes form a ring.

It is called the Ring of Fire.

Are there volcanoes in the United States?

Yes.

Mount St. Helens is in Washington State.
In 1980, it erupted.

This is Mount St. Helens
before it erupted.

This is Mount St. Helens

after it erupted.

Hawaii has the biggest and busiest

volcanoes in the world.

Mauna Loa is the biggest.

Kilauea is the busiest.

(You say them like this:

maw-na LO-a and ki-lo-AY-a.)

Kilauea has been erupting

on and off for 100 years.

It is called

the "drive-in" volcano.

You can drive or even walk

around its giant crater.

Who knows?

You just might see

a lava fire show there!

Can volcanoes do any good?

Yes.

Over time, ash and lava
turn into rich soil.
The soil is good for farming.

Volcanoes also

tell us about the past.

Two thousand years ago,

a volcano erupted in Italy.

It buried the city

of Pompeii under ash.

(You say pom-PAY.)

Now people are digging up Pompeii.

The ash preserved everything—
even the shapes of the people.

Today scientists can usually tell
when a volcano will erupt.
They have special tools.
They watch the movement of the volcano.

They take its temperature.

Sometimes a volcano swells

or the ground gets hot.

Then it is time to watch out!

There are about

500 active volcanoes

in the world.

This map shows

where most of them are found.

"Active" means the volcano

can erupt at any time.

Other volcanoes are inactive.

They have been dead

for thousands of years.

And then there are volcanoes

that are only sleeping.

Now they are quiet.

But who knows when they will wake up?